**This is my younger brother, Cheese . . .**

**and his twin sister, Tomato.**

**We're having a street party for the Queen, but she's not the only one getting crowned!**

**Jeremy Strong** once worked in a bakery, putting the jam into three thousand doughnuts every night. Now he puts the jam in stories instead, which he finds much more exciting. At the age of three, he fell out of a first-floor bedroom window and landed on his head. His mother says that this damaged him for the rest of his life and refuses to take any responsibility. He loves writing stories because he says it is 'the only time you alone have complete control and can make anything happen'. His ambition is to make you laugh (or at least snuffle). Jeremy Strong lives near Bath with his wife, Gillie, three cats and a flying cow.

**www.jeremystrong.co.uk**

## ARE YOU FEELING SILLY ENOUGH TO READ MORE?

THE BEAK SPEAKS
BEWARE! KILLER TOMATOES
CARTOON KID
CHICKEN SCHOOL
DINOSAUR POX
DOCTOR BONKERS! (A Cosmic Pyjamas Adventure)
THE HUNDRED-MILE-AN-HOUR DOG
KRANKENSTEIN'S CRAZY HOUSE OF HORROR
(A Cosmic Pyjamas Adventure)
KRAZY COW SAVES THE WORLD – WELL, ALMOST
LOST! THE HUNDRED-MILE-AN-HOUR DOG
THE HUNDRED-MILE-AN-HOUR DOG GOES FOR GOLD
MY BROTHER'S FAMOUS BOTTOM
MY BROTHER'S HOT CROSS BOTTOM
MY BROTHER'S FAMOUS BOTTOM GETS PINCHED
MY BROTHER'S FAMOUS BOTTOM GOES CAMPING
THERE'S A PHARAOH IN OUR BATH!

JEREMY STRONG'S LAUGH-YOUR-SOCKS-OFF JOKE BOOK
JEREMY STRONG'S LAUGH-YOUR-SOCKS-OFF EVEN MORE JOKE BOOK

# Jeremy STRONG

## My Brother's Famous Bottom Gets Crowned!

**Illustrated by Rowan Clifford**

PUFFIN

PUFFIN BOOKS

Published by the Penguin Group
Penguin Books Ltd, 80 Strand, London WC2R 0RL, England
Penguin Group (USA) Inc., 375 Hudson Street, New York, New York 10014, USA
Penguin Group (Canada), 90 Eglinton Avenue East, Suite 700, Toronto, Ontario, Canada M4P 2Y3
(a division of Pearson Penguin Canada Inc.)
Penguin Ireland, 25 St Stephen's Green, Dublin 2, Ireland (a division of Penguin Books Ltd)
Penguin Group (Australia), 707 Collins Street, Melbourne, Victoria 3008, Australia
(a division of Pearson Australia Group Pty Ltd)
Penguin Books India Pvt Ltd, 11 Community Centre, Panchsheel Park, New Delhi – 110 017, India
Penguin Group (NZ), 67 Apollo Drive, Rosedale, Auckland 0632, New Zealand
(a division of Pearson New Zealand Ltd)
Penguin Books (South Africa) (Pty) Ltd, Block D, Rosebank Office Park, 181 Jan Smuts Avenue, Parktown
North, Gauteng 2193, South Africa

Penguin Books Ltd, Registered Offices: 80 Strand, London WC2R 0RL, England

puffinbooks.com

First published 2013
002

Text copyright © Jeremy Strong, 2013
Illustrations copyright © Rowan Clifford, 2013
All rights reserved

The moral right of the author and illustrator has been asserted

Set in Baskerville
Made and printed in England by Clays Ltd, St Ives plc

British Library Cataloguing in Publication Data
A CIP catalogue record for this book is available from the British Library

ISBN: 978-0-141-34422-5

www.greenpenguin.co.uk

MIX
Paper from
responsible sources
FSC™ C018179
www.fsc.org

Penguin Books is committed to a sustainable
future for our business, our readers and our
planet. This book is made from paper certified
by the Forest Stewardship Council.

ALWAYS LEARNING                    PEARSON

This story is dedicated to bottoms of all kinds –

Fat ones, thin ones, round ones and saggy ones,
Big ones, little ones, red ones and blue,
Happy ones, sad ones, angry ones and baggy ones,
Yellow, green and purple ones and spotty ones too.
Where would we be without them?
*(Standing up, that's where, because you'd*
*have no sit-upon to sit upon.)*

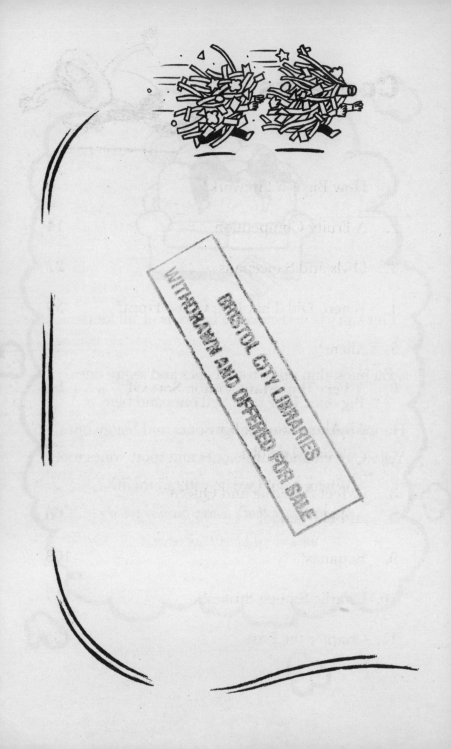

# Contents

## 1. How Big is a Firework?

Mr Tugg has just exploded again, all over our front doorstep. Of course he hasn't *really* exploded, but you know what I mean and you know what he's like. Just in case you don't know I will tell you. He is our next-door neighbour and he is a volcano on legs.

Sometimes he's like this:

And sometimes he's like this:

Guess what made him so angry this time? You're dead right. My dad. My dad is the World Champion at Winding Up Mr Tugg. Let me tell you what happened.

First of all, the front doorbell rang.

*BRRRRRRINNNGGGGGG!*

*BBRRRRIILNNNNNGG!*

'Who can that be?' asked Dad.

Mum looked at him as if he was an idiot. (She does that a lot, because he is!) 'Ron, we can't see through wooden doors. Why don't you answer it and then you'll know.'

'It might be our lovely neighbour, Mr Tugg,' grumbled Dad.

'It might be, but you won't know unless you open that door,' Mum answered.

'You go and see, Brenda.'

'You're not scared of Mr Tugg, are you?' asked Mum as Dad vaulted over the sofa and vanished behind it.

'Silly Daddy!' cried Cheese.

'Silly sausage moo cow!' shouted Tomato.

'Silly sausage moo cow' is her favourite phrase at the moment. Well, you know what three-year-olds are like. Peculiar!

'I'm not scared and I'm definitely not a silly sausage moo cow,' complained an invisible Dad.

In case you're wondering why my little brother and sister are called Cheese and Tomato it's because they were born in the back of a pizza-delivery van and Dad decided they should be named after a pizza. See, I told you my dad's daft. He's the best dad ever!

BRRRINNNNGGGGGGGGGGGGGG! BANG! BANGG!! BANGGG!!!

'It's definitely Mr Tugg.' Dad's muffled voice drifted up from behind the sofa. 'Nobody else makes a noise like that.'

'Oh for heaven's sake,' cried Mum. 'I'll answer it.' Off she went and opened the door and – surprise! There was Mr Tugg.

'Ah,' he said in that annoying voice of his that sounds like a squeezed lemon. 'I knew you were in.'

'Hello, Mr Tugg,' said Mum, showing her best polite smile.

'Silly moo cow!' said Tomato, peeping out from between Mum's legs.

'What did she say?' asked Mr Tugg, and I thought, *Oh dear, here we go. Volcano alert! Prepare for emergency evacuation!*

'Silly sausage moo cow!' Tomato repeated with a nice big smile.

Mr Tugg's eyes narrowed. His nostrils narrowed. Even his brain narrowed. And then, miracle of miracles – he smiled!

'What a darling little child!' he said, even though his teeth were gritted.

'Thank you,' said Mum.

'Boo!' said Cheese, poking *his* head out from behind his sister's.

'Ah, the other one,' said Mr Tugg, sighing. 'Ha ha! Boo to you too, young man.'

My goodness, Mr Tugg was actually being NICE! Amazing! Cheese stuck out his elbows, lifted them up like a pair of wings, filled his little pot belly with air and delivered his speech.

'Boo boo poo poo to you too too too!' Then he ran off behind the sofa, and jumped on top of Dad.

'Get off, you humpy hippo!' puffed Dad.

Mr Tugg peered round the open door. 'Is that your husband behind the sofa? Why is he hiding there?'

Dad groaned and crawled out with Cheese
riding on his back.

'I'm riding a hippopot,' shouted Cheese.

'Not any more you're not,' said Dad, pulling
him off and getting to his feet. 'Ah, Mr Tugg.
How nice to see you.'

'Ffff! Some people might think you were hiding
from me,' whined Mr Tugg. 'First of all nobody
answers the doorbell and then I find you lurking
behind the furniture.'

Dad bowed his head, tugged at his forelock and began speaking with a very strange accent. 'Ah, to be sure, you are always welcome in our 'umble 'ome, sirr, begorra. And will you be partakin' of some Machaggis pie with us, sirrr?'

Mr Tugg's eyebrows were doing a tango across his head. He stared at my mum. 'Is your husband all right?' he asked.

'No, he's mostly all wrong,' Mum quipped, winking at me.

Mr Tugg cleared his throat, pushed back his shoulders and puffed himself up to look as important as possible.

'Now listen here —' he began.

'We be a-listenin', sirr,' Dad went on with his ridiculous Irish-Scottish-Martian accent. 'But what we be a-listenin' for? Is it animal, vegetable or mineral?'

Mr Tugg pushed his shoulders back even more. 'Now look here, I'm on a committee. In fact,' he announced proudly, 'I am the deputy chairman.'

'Oh dear, I'm so sorry,' Dad sympathized in a

more comforting tone. 'I expect you were hoping to be chairman?'

Mr Tugg tried not get huffed. Of course he wanted to be chairman! Mr Tugg would like to be Chairman of the Entire World if possible. He loves committees and feeling important, especially if he's the Chief Big-Wig, which he always is – except this time.

'I'm honoured to be the deputy. The chairman is actually a chairwoman, for your information – Mrs Quince-Porage.'

'Ah,' said Dad, nodding. 'Isn't that the lady up at the big new house with those two great big stone cowpats by her front gate?'

'Cowpats? What are you on about? They're carved stone lions, you idi–' Mr Tugg stopped just in time, clenching his little fists hard. 'Now listen, we have formed a committee to celebrate the sixtieth year of the Queen's coronation and the imminent arrival of the Prince and Princess's twins. We are going to have our very own coronation. We are going to crown the oldest couple in the street as king and queen, AND we are going to let off a firework. There!'

Mr Tugg stepped back proudly.

'A firework?' Mum was puzzled. 'Just one?'

'Yes, but it will be a big one,' promised Mr Tugg.

'How big?' asked Dad.

'Pretty big,' Mr Tugg growled.

'This big?' asked Dad, holding his hand just above the doormat. 'Or this big?' He put his hand on Cheese's head. Cheese looked up at Dad.

'Not a pig!' he interrupted.

'This big?' Dad went on relentlessly. 'This big?' he said, pointing at me. 'This –'

'STOP!' yelled Mr Tugg. 'I don't know how big, you silly, silly man! Just tell me, are you going to help with the street party or not?'

'Ah well, you see, that depends on how big the firework is,' Dad began. 'You see, if it's only this big –' he said, holding his hand over the doormat again, 'or this big –'

'STOP IT! You're driving me mad!'
Oh dear. Dad had definitely lit Mr
Tugg's blue touchpaper and now the
volcano was unstoppable. Mr Tugg
turned red. He turned purple. He went
white, with a touch of green round
his ears. His little feet stamped up and
down. His arms whirled round uselessly.
His eyes bulged and spun like Catherine
wheels. His eyebrows took off and flew
round the room like angry bees. We
stood back and watched in amazement
as Mr Tugg erupted in all directions.

Finally, he calmed down and simply stood there looking limp and spent. What does a volcano do when it's run out of exploding stuff? It looks soggy and miserable, that's what. Mum put a gentle hand on his shoulder.

'Would you like a cup of tea?' she asked. 'People usually do after they meet my husband. Come in and tell us all about your lovely committee and the street party.'

It was a little while before Mr Tugg recovered. Fortunately, he didn't need an ambulance, but he did need three cups of tea, a slice of cake and six custard creams.

'There,' said Mum. 'Feeling better, I hope?'

'Thank you,' nodded Mr Tugg. 'Now then, what I came to ask is whether I can rely on you to help with the food? And, secondly, there is a meeting for everyone at the school hall this evening. We need some good ideas for other things we can do to celebrate the day.'

'Great!' cried Dad. 'We could put a man on the

moon! Or even a small three-year-old child – no, *two* small three-year-olds. Think of the headline – TWINS FOUND ON THE MOON!'

'We will NOT be putting anyone on the moon,' snapped Mr Tugg. 'We are looking for sensible ideas, not utterly ridiculous ones concerning trips into outer space.'

'Shame,' murmured Dad. 'But you can look forward to seeing us at the meeting tonight,' he added. 'We'll have bags of ideas, trolleys full of them, truckloads.' Dad paused and tapped Mr Tugg on the chest with one finger. 'What's bigger than a truck?' he asked.

Mr Tugg groaned and looked at my mum. 'I don't suppose there's any chance you could leave your husband behind the sofa?' he suggested, but Mum just laughed and shook her head.

## 2. A Fruity Competition

The school hall was crowded. Just about everyone from our street was there, plus a few people that weren't, like Granny and her husband, Lancelot, who live just round the corner but had come along for the fun.

Then there was our local policeman, Sergeant Smugg. I don't like him much. He makes you feel that you're always doing something wrong, even when you're not. He's one of those people who like rules and regulations, so I was not surprised to see that Mr Tugg is a good friend of his. Tugg and Smugg – what a pair!

Mrs Quince-Porage was there, of course, because she's the chairperson. She was wearing a very bright dress completely plastered with yellow, blue and red flowers. It looked as if a

14

giant cannon had just blasted
the entire contents of our local
flower shop at her – and they'd
all stuck. *Splip, splap, splop.*

Mrs Q-P was about the
same age as my parents and
she had very blonde hair
piled into a
strange shape
that should
probably have
been a building
rather than a hairstyle.
She was also sporting
gigantic black claw-
like combs above
her eyes, but they
might have been
false eyelashes. They were
so heavy she could barely
keep her eyes open.

She banged on the table in front of her and called for silence in a voice like chocolate boiling over in a saucepan and dribbling down the sides of the cooker.

'GOOD evening, everyone. I am SO glad to see so MANY of you here tonight. Let us get STRAIGHT down to BUSINESS.'

Dad whispered in my ear. 'If that woman's smile gets any bigger her face will split in half and all her teeth will fall out.'

'Shush!' hissed Mum.

'NOW then,' Mrs Quince-Porage continued. 'Has ANYONE got any SUPER suggestions for our CORONATION celebration?'

'Silly sausage moo cow!' shouted Tomato.

'DARLING child!' grinned Mrs Q-P.

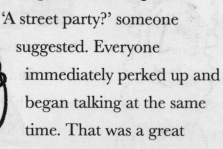

'A street party?' someone suggested. Everyone immediately perked up and began talking at the same time. That was a great idea, what about food? Maybe we could all provide something for the table. Where would the tables come from? The school. What about decorations? And so it went on. Soon it was decided that there would be a fancy-dress competition for the best royal outfit.

'We could make crowns,' my mum told the hall. 'And wear cloaks.'

Dad got to his feet. 'Yes, and we could have executions, like Henry the Eighth, and chop off some heads.'

Most of the audience laughed, but a few people stared at him. Sometimes my dad is a bit embarrassing.

Sergeant Smugg certainly didn't think it was funny. He took it all VERY seriously and said that he wasn't going to allow any executions to take place while he was around. 'I would have to arrest you,' he pointed out.

'It was a joke,' Dad informed the policeman.

'Not to me, it wasn't.' Sergeant Smugg stuck out his chin in an *I-am-determined-to-arrest-all-criminals* kind of way.

'Good,' drooled Mrs Chocolate Voice, ignoring the pair of them. 'Any MORE ideas?'

'What about music and dancing? Maybe we could have a band,' someone suggested.

Dad jumped to his feet again. 'Hey, I'm in a band!'

'Since when have you been in a band?' Mum hissed at Dad.

'Don't say anything,' Dad hissed back. 'It's a band of one at the moment, but Nicholas plays the recorder, don't you? So you're in it for starters.'

I almost choked. 'But I can only do "Three

Blind Mice" –' I began before I was drowned in chocolate by Mrs Quince-Porage.

'And I LOVE singing,' she burbled.

'So do I,' shouted Dad frantically. (That's true, he's always singing, even in his sleep!) 'I AM the singer in the band.'

'And I'M the chairwoman and I WANT to sing so I SHALL,' Mrs Q-P insisted. 'That settles THAT. Any more ideas?'

'How about a beauty competition?' suggested Mr Tugg, blushing rather.

'What's that?' asked Granny, who's a little deaf.

'A fruity competition? Are we making jam?'

There was a ripple of laughter in the hall.

'I said BEAUTY!' shouted Mr Tugg.

'Ooh, thank you dear. Nobody's told me that for years,' Granny answered, leaning across to Lancelot. 'That man with the funny moustache said I'm a beauty.'

Lancelot looked at me and winked. He slipped his arm round Granny's shoulders and gave her a squeeze. Granny looked at me and she winked too! Sometimes I think my whole family are daft. Apart from me, of course.

Mrs Chocolate Voice gave her deputy chairman a withering smile. 'No, no, Mr Tugg. I DO think beauty contests are rather old-fashioned. Besides, this is the age of EQUALITY.'

'Wait a moment!' cried Dad. 'It doesn't have to be a beauty contest for women. Let's have something different. Why not make it a beauty competition for policemen? I think Sergeant

Smugg would
look lovely in a –'

But nobody
could hear what
Dad thought
Sergeant Smugg
would look lovely
in because the whole
hall was howling with
laughter at the very
idea. Everyone except a
rather large and bulky
teenager standing at
the back. His spotty
face was scowling at
everyone, especially my
dad.

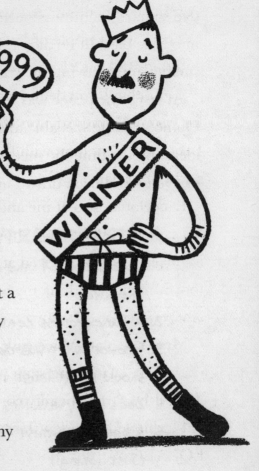

'PLEASE –' dribbled Mrs Quince-Chocolate
or whatever her name is. 'PLEASE –'

'ORDER!' bellowed Mr Tugg, climbing on
to a table. 'ORDER! QUIET!' He glared at my

dad so hard I almost expected Dad to shatter into little bits but he didn't. He simply sat there smiling and enjoying the chaos he'd created.

At last some peace was restored and Mrs Quince-Porage was able to get on with collecting ideas. By the time the meeting was finished a list of events had been drawn up.

## A STREET PARTY

1. Coronation of the oldest couple in the street
2. A fancy-dress contest
3. Fireworks (It was decided that there should be at least three. Whoopee!)
4. Dad's band, with Mrs Q-P as singer
5. A beauty contest for the police (Just joking!)

There was a loud cough from Sergeant Smugg as he cleared his throat and got to his feet. 'Before you all make your way back to your homes, your slippers and pleasant firesides I should just like to say a few words.'

What on earth was he on about? Slippers and pleasant firesides? It wasn't the middle of winter!

Mr Tugg nodded importantly. 'The sergeant wishes to speak.'

'He's already spoken,' Dad called out. 'Get on with it!'

Sergeant Smugg squared his shoulders. 'The road will have to be closed to traffic.'

'Of course the road will be closed to traffic!' shouted Dad. 'How will traffic get past thirty whopping great dining tables going all the way down it?'

The sergeant ignored my dad and went on. 'In addition, I shall have to put up lots of red-and-white tape as a warning.'

'Red-and-white tape,' muttered Dad. 'Jolly good. Must have lots of tape.'

'There must be an official notice for one week

prior to the road closure announcing the closure and a statutory notice handed in to the local police station seven days beforehand signed by someone important, like the Prime Minister.'

'An important man?' Dad's eyes lit up. 'Like Mr Tugg?'

Mr Tugg puffed out his chest at the very idea that he might be important. 'I'm deputy chairman,' he told everyone, but they knew that already of course. 'I could sign it.'

'I'LL sign it,' purred Mrs Quince-Porage. 'I'M the chairwoman.'

Mr Tugg shot an armada of daggers at her.

'Very well,' agreed Sergeant Smugg, consulting his book of rules and regulations. 'In addition, children less than fifty centimetres tall and twenty centimetres wide are not allowed to have balloons in case they are carried away by a tornado.'

'You're mad,' declared Dad.

'Plus, crisps cannot be consumed on the road,' said the policeman.

'Why not?' someone shouted.

'Because they could cause a puncture and they make crumbs,' declared Sergeant Smugg. 'And crumbs attract pigeons, and pigeons make dirty splodges on my police car.'

'But I like crisps!' shouted Lancelot. This was followed by a chorus of 'So do I!' from around the hall.

'I shall arrest any crisp-eaters,' warned the sergeant, 'and apply my handcuffs upon their bodily extremities. That is to say, their wrists.'

'You're definitely mad,' Dad repeated. 'Come on, you lot. Time we went home and left these lunatics to entertain themselves. We've got work to do. I must get the band together and start rehearsing.' Dad rubbed his hands together and grinned. 'I can't wait. We shall probably get to number one in the charts! It's going to be amazing!'

# 3. Owls and Saucepans

Mrs Quince-Porage sings like an owl!

*Question:* Can owls sing?

*Answer:* NO!

I'll tell you what happened. Dad was getting us all together for a rehearsal. Dad's the guitarist and he sings. (At least, he would have sung if Mrs Quince-Porage hadn't turned up and insisted on singing herself.) Mum plays drums. (At least she would have played them if she had any, but she only had some saucepans and wooden spoons.) I played the recorder. (At least I would have but I can only tootle 'Three Blind Mice'.)

We were about to start when who should come to the door? Mrs Quince-Porage herself, and she was very excited.

'I have just had the most WONDERFUL

idea. I was thinking that we REALLY need a SPECIAL PERSON to crown the oldest couple on the street. Now then, I have the most DARLING little niece. She lives right HERE in town and she's GORGEOUS. Sharon Blenkinsop, that's her name and she's fifteen, so JUST the right age. The young shall crown the old. How about THAT! What do you think?!'

Mum nodded. 'It sounds good, but shouldn't the committee be making those decisions?'

Mrs Quince-Porage was astonished. 'But I'M

the chairwoman. I AM the committee!' she
declared.

'I'm sure Mr Tugg will agree,' Mum
murmured and Mrs Q-P rewarded her with such
an intense smile I thought her teeth must be
made of diamonds.

'And now I see you're ready to rehearse, so I
shall SING – tra la la!'

Oh no! Mrs Q-P screeched like an owl!

SKKKKKKKGH!

AAAARRRGGGH!

We were rehearsing in the back room. We had an audience of two, Cheese and Tomato, but even they didn't stay long. The moment they heard us banging and crashing and Mrs Q-P hooting and squawking they fled in search of safety. Even the animals in our back garden were scared silly. I haven't mentioned our animals yet, have I? Here's a list of them:

One tortoise called Schumacher.

One goat called Rubbish.

Captain Birdseye, the cockerel.

Four hens called Mavis Moppet, Beaky,
Leaky and Poop.

Two rabbits called Saucepan and
Nibblewibble.

We've also got beans and lettuce and cabbages and broccoli and courgettes and strawberries – but none of those make any noise. Even so, I bet they were scared too.

Mrs Quince-Porage was DREADFUL! When she sang it was like listening to a million saucepans falling out of her mouth. Not only that but her whole body shook like a jelly on a train. She stood there with her mouth wide open and all those saucepans falling out of it and her

gigantic false eyelashes fluttered up and down so fast I thought they might actually take off and zoom across the room like a pair of big bats.

Phew! It was such a relief when she stopped.

Mrs Q-P opened her eyes wide and gazed around the room. 'What DO you think?' she asked.

Mum was pressing her wooden spoons over her ears. Dad was lying flat on his back as if he was dead. I was on the sofa with a cushion over my head.

Mum lowered the spoons. 'I think we'll stop there for today. We'll let you know when the next practice is.'

'LOVELY,' beamed Mrs Q-P. 'I enjoyed that. I don't often get the chance to SING.'

'I'm not surprised,' muttered Dad.

'I BEG your pardon?'

'I said I was surprised,' Dad said, choking. 'By your voice. It's quite – something.'

'Thank you!' Mrs Quince-Porage was delighted and went marching out of the house humming a tune tunelessly. Mum and Dad stared after her.

'What are we going to do?' asked Dad. 'That was the worst singing I have ever heard. That woman could sink ships with a voice like that.'

'She was very bad,' agreed Mum. 'And, to tell you the truth, Ron, we weren't all that good either. Banging pots and pans is ridiculous.'

'Don't worry. I'll get you a proper set of drums,' Dad told her. 'I'll make one.'

Mum looked at Dad for a moment and then

burst into hysterical laughter. 'YOU! MAKE a set of DRUMS!?'

'Funny Daddy!' shouted Tomato, who had come creeping back into the room with Cheese, now that the singing saucepan factory (Mrs Q-P!) had gone home.

Mum heaved a sigh. 'Listen, if we are going to make this band work we need help. For a start we need proper instruments and proper musicians. What with my pots and pans, Mrs Q-P's singing and Nicholas's 'Three Blind Mice', we were totally hopeless. If we play like that at the coronation we'll probably have rotten eggs thrown at us.'

My brain suddenly lit up. 'Maybe Granny and Lancelot can help? Lancelot used to play the saxophone and I know he's still got it because he showed me and he played a tune and it wasn't 'Three Blind Mice', it had loads of notes in it. Maybe Granny used to play something too.'

'Yes, she plays the fool,' grumbled Dad.

'You can talk!' declared Mum. 'I think
Nicholas's suggestion is very sensible.
Thank heavens there are two sensible
people in this family.'

'Two?' repeated Dad.

'Yes, me and Nicholas. Don't ever think
you're one of them. The hens have got
more sense than you.'

'*Pwarrk!*' clucked Dad. '*Pwark-pwark-pwarrrrkkk!*' He began strutting round the room doing a chicken impression until we had tears rolling down our cheeks.

'Silly sausage poo hen!' yelled Tomato, and we all joined Dad, elbows out, strutting and clucking. *Pwarrkkk! Pwark!* Up and over the sofa, bouncing on the armchairs. *Pwaarrrkk!*

Dad suddenly came to a dead stop and he whirled round. 'Nicholas, you know what you said about Granny playing an instrument? You could be on to something. You'd better nip round to their house and see what they have to say. I think you might be in for a surprise.'

Then he stuck his fists into his armpits and off he went once more. 'Come on, my chicken-army! Left – *pwarrkkk*! Right – *pwarrkkk*!'

# 4. Where Did That Dog Come From?

Granny and Lancelot only live about five minutes walk from us so I zipped round there and told them everything.

Lancelot laughed and straightened his long grey ponytail. 'We know all about Mrs Quince-Porage, don't we, babe?'

Urrrgh! I don't know why Lancelot insists on calling my granny 'babe'. I mean, she's at least sixty-four. That's almost a hundred!

'Mrs Quince-Porage?' said Granny. 'Oh yes. We've heard her singing. It sounds to me like a pig being hit on the nose with a rolling pin. She sings in her bath with the window open. What's more, her garden backs on to ours so we can hear every squawk.'

'We've got to drown her out by making lots

of noise with the other instruments,' I said. 'I thought Lancelot could play his saxophone. Did you used to play anything, Granny?'

Granny stared ahead rather dreamily and nodded. 'Oh yes. I was in a pop group.'

My granny? In a band? I almost fell off my chair in disbelief.

'Really? Wow! I mean, when?'

'A very long time ago, almost fifty years,' sighed Granny.

Fifty years ago! That was probably before the Romans. I gave Granny a nice smile and asked her if that was when the dinosaurs were on earth.

'NO IT WAS NOT, you cheeky whatsit!' she cried.

I shook my head. 'Granny, I can't believe you were ever in a pop group.'

'Oh it's true, Nicholas. You see, when you youngsters look at old people all you see is how old they are. You forget that old people were young once and wanted to do all the exciting things you like doing. You know Mrs Wibbly, that old lady in your street? She's eighty-seven, but I happen to know that she got a gold medal for the pole vault at the 1952 Olympic Games.'

'That's amazing! But, Gran, when you were in your pop group what instrument did you play?'

'The double bass.'

This time I really did fall off my chair. The double bass!

'But, Granny, you're too small to play the double bass!'

Granny gave me such a dirty look. 'Nicholas, I'll have you know that I was the best double bass player for miles around. I was almost on television once.'

Lancelot frowned at her. 'I thought that was because you fell in the river.'

'Well, yes, I did fall in the river but I was playing the double bass when it happened and it fell in with me. It was so funny, Nicholas. I wish you'd been there. You see, the band was playing on a boat. We got a bit carried away and I was doing my usual thing –'

'I think you'd better tell Nicholas what your "usual thing" was, babe,' prompted Lancelot.

Aarrrrgh! That 'babe' business again. I can't stand it!

Granny's eyes were shining. 'I didn't just *play*

the double bass. I used
it like a piece of gym
equipment. Sometimes
I stood on the side of it
and jumped off. I would
swing it about and whirl
it round. I balanced on
it. And this particular
day I lost my footing on
the boat and the double
bass and I both fell over
the edge. We made
quite a splash I can tell
you. I had to paddle
ashore, sitting on it!'

I looked at my gran.
She seemed so small
and sweet and kind.
Who'd have thought
she once used a double
bass as a canoe?

'Have you still got your bass?' I asked.

'It's upstairs in a wardrobe. It used to have a proper case but I chopped that up and burned it one winter when we were cold. But I could never burn my bass and, anyhow, it was still a bit wet from going in the river.'

Lancelot and I followed Granny upstairs. In the back bedroom was a big wardrobe with double doors. Granny opened them up and there was the double bass. It was the most battered thing I had ever seen, covered in large bits of tape like giant plasters. It had actual holes in it too, with splintered edges. It looked as if it had fought the whole of World War Two on its own.

'As you can see, Nicky, it's been much loved,' Granny said with a rather wicked grin on her face. 'Oooh, I can't wait to get my fingers plucking those strings again!'

She lifted the bass out of the wardrobe, placed one hand on the neck and slowly began to twang the strings. A quick bit of tuning and then Granny was off. *Plink! Plonk! Plunk! Twang!* Faster and faster went her fingers, her feet began to jiggle up and down and suddenly she pulled a huge thunking *TWONNGGGG!* on the lowest string, leaped in the air and ended up balancing with one foot on the curving side and the free arm and leg sticking out into the air. Granny jumped back down, a huge beaming smile on her face.

'There! What do you think of that?'

'Fantastic, Gran. But I can see how you might end up falling into a river.'

They both laughed.

'Fantastic is the word, Nicholas,' said Lancelot. 'Don't you think my babe's the best ever? You tell your dad that we'll be at your house tomorrow for band practice. Wouldn't miss it for the world. We're going to make so much noise Mrs Q-P will think there's an earthquake. She'll run straight back home and hide under the table.'

I left Granny's house feeling on top of the world. Mum and Dad would be really pleased when they heard the good news. We now had at least two proper musicians in the band. Maybe Dad would say I didn't need to be in it any more. After all, who wants to hear 'Three Blind Mice' being played on a recorder at a street party? No one, that's who.

I had almost reached my house when I heard loud shouts from behind.

'Nick! Watch out!'

I was just turning round to see who
it was when I caught sight of a flash of
black and I was completely bowled off
my feet. I crashed to the ground, rolling
on to my back. Before I could even try
to get up the creature was upon me,
nudging me with a wet black nose and
occasionally giving me a good going
over with its wash-flannel tongue.

A boy came pounding up to me, still yelling. 'Streaker! You daft dog! Leave Nicholas alone. Sorry, Nick, Streaker's a bit of a handful. She just about pulled my arm off when she saw you and I had to let go of the lead. Are you OK?'

It was Trevor. He's in my class at school and his dog is kind of famous in our town. What I mean is that Streaker is famous for being a nuisance, although she's hugely friendly too – as you can

tell by the fact that she carried on cleaning me all over even when I was back on my feet.

'I'm fine, and I've had a free wash too. What's all the fuss about? Why all the shouting?'

'I wanted to warn you. Bad news. You know that meeting about the street party? Charlie Smugg was there.'

My face fell. I'd never seen Charlie, but I'd heard lots about him. He's a bit of a bully and he likes to spoil any bit of fun going. He also happens to be the son of Sergeant Smugg, our local policeman, which makes him doubly difficult to deal with.

'Was he the pimply pudding standing at the back?' I asked.

Trevor nodded. 'He came up to me today and said we'd all better watch out. He's got plans, he said. His exact words were – "Your street party is history. It's not going to happen. You wait and see." Then he went off with his three Alsatians in tow, laughing his spotty face off.'

We looked at each other. This was serious. What was Charlie Smugg planning to do? And why? By the time I got back home I was well and truly WORRIED.

## 5. Aliens!

We've been making crowns today. I'd
been awake half the night fretting
about Charlie Smugg, so making
crowns this morning took my mind
off my problems. Dad had gone
out to do something important,
but he wouldn't say what.

Mum cleared the dining-
room table and piled it high
with coloured paper, bits of
old giftwrap from Christmas
and birthdays, thin card,
thick card, foil, glue,
scissors, pens and pencils,
and anything else she could
think of that might be useful.

Granny and Lancelot came down to help the twins. Well, they *said* they were helping the twins, but really they wanted to make crowns for themselves.

Granny kept testing her crown out for size, popping it on and off her head and making Cheese giggle.

'Granny, your crown looks wonky!'

'I look like a monkey?' Granny squeaked in horror. 'I do NOT! Nicholas, do I look like a monkey?'

'No, Gran. Cheese said your crown is WONKY – and it is.' I tried to straighten it for her.

Granny shook her head and wagged a finger at Cheese. 'You should learn to speak more clearly,' she told him.

Lancelot raised one eyebrow. 'And I think *you* should learn to listen more carefully, babe. Your poor hearing gets you into trouble.'

Granny looked daggers at her husband, picked up a huge pile of paper and pushed it across the table to him.

'What's all this for?' Lancelot asked.

Granny's eyes narrowed. 'It's for you to keep your thoughts wrapped up in so nobody else has to know about them!' she shot back, and we all fell about laughing, except for Cheese and Tomato who didn't understand. They just grinned madly and searched our faces for clues as to what was going on.

'Silly saus–' Tomato started, but Mum clapped a hand over her mouth. 'If I hear that phrase one more time I'm sure I shall explode,' she complained.

'BANG!' yelled Cheese, and then fell about. 'Mummy exploded-ded!'

'Exploded,' I corrected.

Cheese looked at me for a moment and then said, slowly, 'Exploded-ded-ded-ded-ded-ded–' until I had to put a hand over *his* mouth. He is SO cheeky.

'We could make crowns for the animals,' I suggested. 'Then they could join in the procession before the street party.'

Mum thought for a few moments. 'Hmmm. A crown for a tortoise. Would that work? Probably not. Schumacher doesn't exactly travel fast either. And the chickens – you'll never get them to walk in a straight line. The rabbits will go bouncing off in all directions, as they do.'

Mum was right, unfortunately. If Schumacher the tortoise joined the procession it would probably take weeks just to walk the length of our road. But there was one animal left. Rubbish, the goat. She was perfect.

'OK, I have had another idea and it's even better,' I announced proudly. 'Rubbish could wear a crown and pull a little cart. We could put the chickens on the cart, or maybe even the twins.'

'Where would we get a cart from?' asked Mum.

'I've got a cart,' Lancelot said.

'Have you, dear?' Granny was surprised. 'I've never seen it.'

'Ah, that's because it's actually a large wheelbarrow at the moment. What I shall do is tie a long pole to each of the handles to make shafts for the cart. It's as simple as that.'

Granny beamed at her husband. 'My knight in shining armour! You are so clever sometimes, I could kiss you.'

'You could kiss me anyway,' said Lancelot. 'Why hang about?'

'Granny! Lancelot! Behave!' I shouted.

'Oh dear, the poor boy's embarrassed,' murmured Granny. And do you know what she did? She stretched across the table, put her hands firmly on my cheeks, yanked me towards her and gave ME the biggest, wettest kiss EVER!

URRRGH! GIANT SQUID ATTACK!!

'There. Now I bet you'd much rather I'd kissed

Lancelot, don't you?' she said, but by that time
I had slid under the table and was lying there
pretending to be dead.

Mum was thinking out loud. 'This cart
business. Let's get this straight. The band is
on stage and we are all in the band. So who is
looking after Rubbish? She won't walk along by
herself. Someone will need to lead her in the
parade.'

Oh dear, a bit of a problem. Or maybe not.

'I could ask Trevor,' I suggested.

'Is he any good with animals?' Granny wanted
to know.

'Yes,' I said, keeping my fingers crossed. After
all, Trevor's dog, Streaker, wasn't known as the
Hundred-Mile-an-Hour-Dog for nothing. There
was that time when she managed to knock over
the town's Christmas tree and all the Christmas
lights, not to mention the time she ate all the pies
from a van. Then there was the time she widdled
in the middle of the dog show, and the time she –

hmmmm! It was quite a long list, so I kept quiet.

'Next time you see Trevor ask him and see if he can,' Mum said.

We eventually finished making our crowns. Mum's looked totally royal. It was silver and gold, with lots of pointy bits and glossy red and green jewels stuck round the edges.

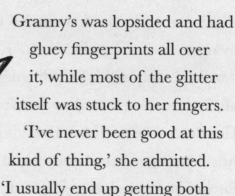

Granny's was lopsided and had gluey fingerprints all over it, while most of the glitter itself was stuck to her fingers.

'I've never been good at this kind of thing,' she admitted. 'I usually end up getting both hands stuck together. Oh dear, I just have. Lancelot, help me pull my hands apart. Oh, now you're stuck to me. We're glued together!'

But I think Cheese and Tomato had done the best ones. They had made the craziest crowns ever, although I'm not sure 'crown' is the best word for them. Basically, they had made two headbands from card and then stuck shapes on them.

The rest of us had cut things out too – diamonds, triangles, circles, squares and so on, but the twins' shapes were shapeless! They were blobby and loopy or twirly or flappy. They looked like jelly when you drop it on the floor, and they came in all colours. Some were made of card so they were stiff. Others were all floppy.

The twins had made MILLIONS of them. Then they had stuck EVERY SINGLE ONE of those shapes on to their headbands. When Cheese and Tomato put those crowns on their heads you couldn't actually see the twins at all. Great long streamers of Christmas wrapping paper and flippy-flappy bits of foil spiralled down to their knees. Prongy things stuck up into the air and all you could see were two rather weird creatures, with three-year-old legs sticking out at the bottom.

'I'm not sure the twins have actually made crowns,' murmured Mum. 'Unless aliens from a very strange universe wear crowns like that.'

Unfortunately, Cheese couldn't see where he was going and he walked straight into the door instead of through it. Lancelot grabbed a couple of toilet rolls and stuck them together to make a pair of binoculars so Cheese could look through them and not bash into things. The twins wandered out to the back garden to show off their creations to Rubbish and the other animals.

Shortly after that Dad came back from wherever he'd been and he was almost jumping with excitement. He grabbed Mum's shoulders and looked at her with blazing eyes.

'You will never guess what I have got for you, Brenda!'

Mum was immediately worried, as well she should. 'You're right, Ron. I will never guess, because the sort of things you usually bring home for me are often so, so – how shall I say this? – BIZARRE. Do you remember Crunchbag the alligator? It's not another alligator, is it? I don't think I could cope with another alligator.'

'Stop being such a meany and listen. I have got you – A PROPER DRUM KIT!'

Mum actually squealed and clapped her hands! She did a little dance. She grabbed Dad and waltzed him round the room. 'A proper drum kit! That is wonderful, darling! But how? How did you do it?'

'Well,' began Dad breezily, 'I just went into

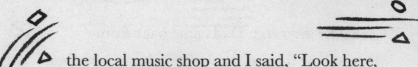

the local music shop and I said, "Look here, we're having a street party with a procession and a crowning ceremony and there's going to be a terrific number-one band playing, but we need a drum kit so why don't you lend us one and it will be a great advert for your shop because we'll tell everyone the kit came from you." And the shop said, "All right, you're on." So there we are. Simple.'

Mum kissed him. 'Thank you,' she said. 'A proper drum kit. That's wonderful.'

It was all very exciting. It was even more exciting when the twins came rushing back into the house to show Dad their crowns.

He took one look at them, threw his arms up in horror and bolted from the room.

'Help! Aliens! Run for your lives! Aliens! Run!'

He fled at top speed down the front path and away up the road, waving his arms furiously at hooting cars and scattering surprised people in all directions. 'Run!' he screamed. 'Aliens! All the way from outer space!'

Behind him came the twins, almost tripping over all those scraps dangling from their crowns. 'Come back, Daddy! It's us!'

The three of them vanished round the corner. Mum gazed after them for a bit and then smiled. 'Peace and quiet at last. Isn't it lovely? Anyone for a cup of tea?'

## 6. A Very Important Visitor, Sort Of

The Band had another practice today. It was the first one with Granny and Lancelot AND the proper drum kit. Dad said we should have a proper name for ourselves. 'The Fab Four,' he suggested, but Mum shook her head.

'I've heard that somewhere before. Besides, there are five of us.'

Dad looked surprised and did a head count. 'Nope, four,' he repeated.

'Five,' said Mum. 'You've forgotten our wonderful singer, Mrs Quince-Porage.'

Dad groaned. 'Of course. I deliberately didn't ask her to the rehearsal.'

'She'll find out sooner or later,' Mum warned.

'That woman will ruin our band,' Dad insisted. 'We shall have to call ourselves The Feeble

Weebles or something like that. Can't we ship her off to the Antarctic? Or maybe we could nail up all the doors in her house so she can't get out and then she'll have to stay indoors and we can get on with everything. We can't let her sing. Her voice is terrible. If we let her loose at the street party and she opens her mouth people will die! She'll screech them to death. There'll be hundreds of dead lying in the road!'

Cheese threw himself on the floor. 'Look, Daddy, I'm dead-ed-ed!'

'Just dead,' Mum laughed. 'Not dead-ed-ed.'

I bet you know what Cheese did next. He lay on the floor, looked cheekily at Mum and slowly said, 'Dead-ed-ed-ed-ed-ed-ed-ed-ed-ed-ed-ed-ed-ed-ed-ed-ed-ed-ed–'

'You will be in a minute, if you don't stop,' Dad threatened, interrupting him.

'And I'm dead-ed-ed too!' Tomato shouted, wanting to join in the fun.

'But you're standing up,' Dad pointed out.

'How can you
be dead standing
up?'

'Because,
because –' she
began. 'I'm a
dead-ed fish
finger!'

Dad looked at
Mum and held
up his hands.
'What is she
talking about?'

Mum smiled. 'It's simple. She's saying she's a
frozen fish finger, and that's why she can stand
up. She's frozen stiff.'

Dad glanced at Tomato and then back at Mum
and the rest of us. He shook his head hard as if
he was trying to get rid of something that was
bothering him.

Granny had been quietly picking at her

double-bass strings. 'Please can we get on with the rehearsal? That's what we are here for. We can call ourselves The Bouncing Bandits, because "bandits" has the word "band" in it, and I'm going to do a lot of bouncing.'

'You won't bounce into the river, Gran, will you?' I asked.

'No, Nicholas, I shan't. Now then, after me — a-one, a-two, a-three, four, five and —'

We launched into a really rocking song and for the first time we sounded great. Mum's drumming was terrific, and everyone did well, except for me. I'm not sure my squeaky version of 'Three Blind Mice' on the recorder added much. Lancelot winked at me halfway through and at the end he took me to one side.

'Come up to our place tomorrow. I'll write out the tunes for you and show you where the notes are on the recorder and then you can practise a bit.'

'Thanks, Lancelot,' I grinned. 'I thought I sounded a bit odd.'

Just then there was a loud banging on the front door. I opened it and there was Mr Tugg.

'Are you aware of the noise you have been making?' he demanded, already bright red round the ears and looking dangerous.

Dad was just about to speak to him when Granny pushed past and confronted Mr Tugg herself.

'And are YOU aware of to whom you are speaking?' Granny demanded crossly, looking Mr Tugg up and down as if he was a piece of dirty rubbish someone had thrown out of their car.

Mr Tugg squinted at Granny. He obviously thought he'd seen her before, but he wasn't absolutely sure. Before he could even open his mouth, Granny went on.

'I am Lady Gaga, the famous singer.'

Mr Tugg's eyebrows almost took off. 'Lady Gaga? But surely she's much younger than you?'

Granny straightened up and glared back at Mr Tugg. 'Are you suggesting I look old?'

'It's just that I thought Lady –'

'You didn't think at all!' cried Granny. 'I suppose you do know what make-up is? Before I go on stage I transform myself. Utterly. It's almost as if I become someone I'm not. Now please go away and stop disturbing me. I am here to practise with my favourite band, The Bouncing Bandits. You must have heard of them.'

Mr Tugg peered past Granny's shoulder at Dad and Mum and Lancelot. 'They're a famous band?' he asked in disbelief. His moustache was wriggling uncomfortably all over his upper lip.

'The best,' Granny said firmly. 'And now we need to get on with our rehearsal. Please go back to your little house, little man and let us get on with it.' And with that she pushed the door shut.

We were all breathing a sigh of relief when then there was another, rather timid knock at the door. Granny opened it and there was Mr Tugg again.

'Who did you say you were?' he croaked.

'Lady Gogo, I mean, I'm Gaga.' Granny declared. 'For heaven's sake go away!'

Mr Tugg held out a piece of paper. 'Could I have your autograph?' he squeaked.

'There,' said Granny, scribbling away. 'Bye-bye!' She shut the door once more.

Granny leaned back against the wall and smiled at us. 'Right then, countdown from five, ready? Five, four, three, two, one . . .'

And on zero we all fell about laughing. It was hilarious. We were still rolling about when there was a third knock at the door. We froze on the spot. Mum peeped through the side window.

'It's Mr Tugg AND Mrs Quince-Porage!' she hissed.

Granny clutched her head in a complete dither. 'What now?'

'You go upstairs and hide,' Mum ordered. 'We'll sort things out down here.'

Granny scurried upstairs while we grabbed our instruments and pretended to be busy. Dad opened the door.

'Sorry to bother you again,' said Mr Tugg, 'but I told Mrs Quince-Porage that Lady Gaga is with you and she is one of her greatest fans and would love to meet her.'

'Yes I WOULD,' drooled Mrs Quince-Porage. 'She's my IDOL, my STAR singer.' Mrs Q-P made Lady Gaga sound like her favourite chocolate.

'I'm afraid she's not here,' said Dad.

'But she was here just a moment ago,' said Mr Tugg, rather puzzled. 'Where is she?'

'She's hiding upstairs!' piped Tomato, poking her head between Dad's legs.

Dad pushed her back behind him. 'What Tomato means is that Lady Gaga *was* upstairs. She had to go to the little room, you know? But then she had to catch the bus home because she'd left the oven on.'

'The BUS?' yelped Mrs Quince-Porage. 'Lady Gaga on a BUS? I would have thought she'd have a ROLLS-ROYCE.'

'She did, but it got a puncture,' Dad said inventively and he turned to Tomato. 'Why don't you show Mrs Quince-Porage your frozen fish-finger impression?'

But Mrs Quince-Porage wasn't interested in Tomato's fish-finger impression. Her eyes were staring at the instruments we were holding.

'Are you rehearsing?' she asked, her eyes lighting up.

Dad opened his mouth, but no sound would come out. He just could not think what to say. Yes? No? Maybe? Would any of them make any difference? No, not at all, because Mrs Q-P was already pushing past Mr Tugg and into our house.

'Excellent,' she drooled. 'I was thinking ONLY this morning when I got up that we REALLY ought to have a rehearsal and here you are ALL ready and waiting. Right ho, let's get on with it!'

We dragged ourselves into the back room and there was Granny's double bass, lying on its side, covered with plasters and full of holes.

'Goodness, that double bass has seen better days' said Mrs Quince-Porage.

'It's only just come out of hospital,' murmured Dad and Mrs Q-P shot him a look.

'Hospital?'

'Yes. It had an operation, a double heart transplant.'

'Oh,' smiled Mrs Q-P. 'I get it. You're being funny! Now, WHICH song shall we do FIRST?'

'How about "March of the Dead"?' suggested Dad, and Mrs Q-P turned to Mum.

'Your husband is SUCH a comedian. I just LOVE his sense of humour.'

Dad groaned. 'I think I'll join Tomato and do fish-finger impressions for the rest of the day,' he grunted.

So we rehearsed and it was awful. Mrs Quince-Porage sounded like an elephant slowly being squeezed by a giant python while having got a pair of bagpipes stuck halfway down its trunk.

The twins went and hid under their beds. The
animals in the back garden huddled together
at the far end in a trembling heap, trying to get
as far away from the noise as possible. Even the
tortoise was up there, with his legs and head
pulled firmly beneath his shell.

We were all relieved when we stopped and Mrs Quince-Porage went home. Dad slumped into a chair. Lancelot packed away his saxophone in silence. Granny and Mum hugged each other, and held on tightly as if they had heard something utterly terrifying.

'It can't go on,' muttered Dad. 'WE can't go on. SHE can't go on! We have to do something.'

## 7. All About Boring Biros, Falls and Tumbles

This morning I went up to Granny's house. Lancelot has written out all the music for me to play on my recorder. All I have to do now is practise it. Lots. It's a relief not to have to tootle 'Three Blind Mice' any more. Lancelot told me about improvizing. That's when you don't just play the tune, you play *around* the tune. It sort of sounds like the tune, but it isn't. He showed me on his saxophone and it looked easy, but I'm not sure it is.

I had no idea he and Granny were musicians. Granny was right when she said we don't know what people can do until they show us. I mean, Mrs Wibbly might be eighty-seven now, but once upon a time she got a gold medal – at the

Olympics! Pole-vaulting! I don't suppose she can jump over her front doorstep now. That makes me feel a bit sad. I guess she'll always have her gold medal, though.

When I got back home Mum asked me to take the twins up to the play area in the park.

'They're getting under my feet,' she complained. 'And they need some fresh air.'

The play area has got lots of climbing stuff – a slide, swings for big children, swings for little children, a zip wire and a kind of wooden thing with platforms and little cabins at each end.

The twins love it and they had great fun chasing each other round and round.

I sat on top of the big slide and watched the world go by. After a while I noticed a large lumpy person trying to balance on a skateboard while throwing tennis balls for his three Alsatians. I watched them for about a minute, wondering if he'd fall off and then suddenly I realized who it was. CHARLIE SMUGG. I immediately wanted to grab the twins and creep away but he had already spotted me. He stuck his skateboard under one arm, called his dogs and headed straight for me.

I don't know why people have to have more than one dog, especially Alsatians. I mean, why three? One is pretty terrifying. I asked Dad about it once and he said that people with big dogs are usually scared of something themselves and they have big scary dogs so they can pretend that they're not. I thought Dad was joking, because he usually is. But he wasn't. He was being serious.

Anyhow, Charlie Smugg looks scary to me. I've never seen so many spots on a face. It's like the moon. His three dogs were snarling and snapping at their leads. He scowled up at me on the slide and kept throwing a tennis ball into the air and catching it. Up − catch, up − catch. There was something about the way he did it that made it seem strange, as if it was some kind of secret message.

'Enjoying yourself?' he sneered.

'Yes,' I answered, trying to sound brave and challenging, but my voice came out all squeaky like my recorder playing.

He began to laugh: an unpleasant, low laugh. He put his skateboard on the path, looked up at me and said, 'See you, sucker,' and slowly scooted off, still laughing to himself.

Phew! I'd escaped. But what was all that about?

I took the twins back home and found Mum and Dad puzzling over a letter that they had found on the doormat. It had no stamp on it so someone must have put it through the letterbox. Inside the envelope was a single sheet of paper. There was a message made of letters cut from a newspaper.

StOp thE cRowNiNg
OR thEr WiL bE tRubBel!!

'What does it mean?' asked Mum.

Dad grunted. 'It means that whoever sent this can't spell, that's what it means. It's just some kid trying to make mischief.'

Guess what I was thinking? I reckoned I knew

that kid, only he wasn't so much a kid as a lumpy, moon-cratered teenager. I didn't say anything because I was only guessing. Besides, at that time I couldn't imagine why Charlie Smugg would want to stop a party. I mean, it was going to be fun!

Later that afternoon there was another committee meeting, called by Mr Tugg of course.

'I'm afraid Mrs Quince-Porage can't be with us today but I've called this meeting to bring you all up to date,' he began in his lemon-juice whine. 'Going through our list of events we have one new item, a procession along the road to help get

everything going. This will be a chance to show
off fancy-dress costumes and crowns, all fitting in
with the royal theme. At the same time prizes will
be awarded for the best fancy dress.'

'Will you be in fancy dress, Mr Tugg?' Dad
piped up.

Mr Tugg reddened and shook his head. 'I am
deputy chairman, it would be beneath my dignity
to dress up.'

'Never mind,' said Dad. 'Just come as a
volcano. You don't need to dress for that.'

Mum dug her elbow into Dad's side. 'Stop it,
Ron!'

'He gets up my nose,' Dad snapped back. 'He's such a miserable meany.'

'The procession will be followed by the crowning of the oldest couple in the street and I am very pleased to announce that they are Mr and Mrs Wibbly.'

'Three cheers!' someone shouted and several hoorays rang out.

'It is my pleasure to tell you that Sharon Blenkinsop, Mrs Quince-Porage's niece, has agreed to do the crowning ceremony. Sharon will be representing the young people of our town, so we shall have young and old on stage. During the crowning The Bouncing Bandits will be playing.'

'Hooray!' shouted Dad.

'Shush,' hissed Mum.

'That will be followed by the party and then dancing in the street with more music from the band. I am sure you will be pleased to learn that The Bouncing Bandits are a group favoured by none other than Lady Gaga – and I have her autograph!'

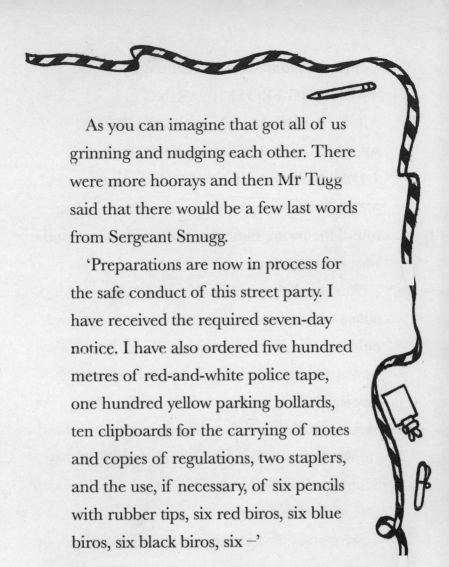

As you can imagine that got all of us grinning and nudging each other. There were more hoorays and then Mr Tugg said that there would be a few last words from Sergeant Smugg.

'Preparations are now in process for the safe conduct of this street party. I have received the required seven-day notice. I have also ordered five hundred metres of red-and-white police tape, one hundred yellow parking bollards, ten clipboards for the carrying of notes and copies of regulations, two staplers, and the use, if necessary, of six pencils with rubber tips, six red biros, six blue biros, six black biros, six —'

'I'M DYING!' Dad suddenly yelled.
'I'M DYING FROM HEARING
ABOUT TOO MANY BORING BIROS!
AAAAAARRRRRGGGGGHHH!'

Dad slumped back into his chair and pretended to be dead. A ripple of laughter ran round the room, but Sergeant Smugg was not the least bit amused.

'It is my duty to make the public aware of police activity in this area and what the general public may expect,' he said, sniffing. 'I must also warn you that dancing is a dangerous activity, especially if the surface is wet. Public taking part in dancing activities should make sure they are wearing the correct clothing, namely sturdy boots, knee and elbow pads and crash helmets, in case of a fall or tumble.'

Somebody in the audience called out, 'I'm not wearing a crash helmet to dance, you pompous numbskull!'

Dad waved a mischievous hand in the air.

'Yes?' asked Sergeant Smugg rather suspiciously.

'Could you please tell us the difference between a fall and a tumble?' asked Dad innocently. He got to his feet. 'You see, I'm confused. Suppose *this* happens to me –'

Dad pretended to slip to the floor. He lay at the sergeant's feet and gazed up at him. 'Would that be a fall, or a tumble?'

'That's a fall,' the sergeant announced.

'Right, so if *this* happens –' Dad got up and promptly fell down again. 'Is that a tumble?'

'That's another fall,' the policeman declared.

Dad sat up. 'Oh, it felt like a tumble to me.'

'It was a fall,' insisted Sergeant Smugg.

'In that case, could you show us exactly what a tumble looks like?' asked Dad.

The poor policeman at last realized that Dad was just winding him up. He huffed and puffed and finally said there were more important things to do.

'I understand that fireworks will be deployed at the end of the evening. Rockets must not be held in the hand or given to small children under one metre in height or less than thirty centimetres wide. While watching fireworks on the ground goggles should be worn and it is advisable that anyone watching should stay indoors and pull the curtains shut.'

'I've had enough of this nonsense,' said Dad.

'I'm going home. Come on.'

Everyone left, apart from Sergeant Smugg and Mr Tugg. The policeman carried on explaining things to Mr Tugg, who sat and listened and nodded. Funny how much they are like each other. Smugg and Tugg. They've both got silly moustaches. They both love rules and regulations. Anyhow, I expect they're still there.

## 8. I Meet the King and Queen
   – and Hartlepool

Mum's been busy sewing all morning. It's not
something she does often so it's taken her a while.
She's been making royal cloaks for Mr and Mrs
Wibbly to wear when they get crowned king and
queen of our street.

Mum had to get the sewing machine working
first. She stared at it for several minutes
wondering what to do. Dad didn't help. He
walked past with the twins in tow, saw her gazing
at it and asked if she was trying to find where to
put the petrol in.

'No, Ron. It's a sewing machine, not a car. Why
don't you do something useful with the twins?
That would be helpful. We need to make some
food for the street party and I'm running behind.

They could help you make some sausage rolls.'

Dad tugged his beard thoughtfully. 'Hmmm, how do you make a sausage roll?' he asked.

'Take it to the top of a hill and let go?' I suggested.

'Boom-Boom!' cried Dad, and Cheese giggled madly.

'Silly sausage roll moo cow!' He wriggled about on the floor, kicking his legs. I think it was meant to be an impression of a sausage rolling down a hill. (It was almost as good as Tomato's fish-finger impression!)

'I live in a mad-house,' muttered Mum, still fiddling with the sewing machine.

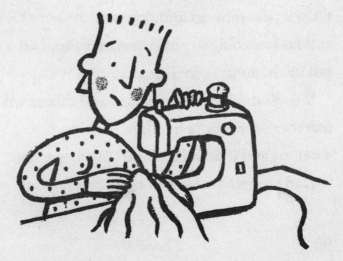

'OK, come on, you two terrors. Let's help Mummy and hit the kitchen,' said Dad, and off they went.

I turned to Mum. 'Are you sure it's a good idea to let Dad AND the twins loose in the kitchen?'

'I don't have any choice,' she answered. 'I must get these cloaks finished. Maybe you could help too and make sure they don't get carried away?'

As it happened, Dad had decided not to make sausage rolls. He thought making mini pizzas would be easier.

'Because they can make their own toppings for the pizzas,' he explained.

'I'm going to put cheese on mine!' shouted Cheese, jumping up and down.

'And I'm going to put strawberry jam and salami on mine,' said Tomato.

'I don't think strawberry jam and salami will go together very well,' I told her.

'All right, I'll do salami and blackberry jam.'

Dad cleared the kitchen table and got out

the flour and some water and yeast
to make the pizza dough. The twins
stood on chairs and Dad showed them
what to do and they began work.

Before you could say 'Get me out
of here!' the kitchen was BURSTING
with clouds of flour dust. Flour was
everywhere. It was a flour tornado. I
mean, the twins are small and there
are only two of them. How could they
possibly make so much mess?

'I can't see a thing!' cried Dad,
peering through the flour fog.

'This is fun!' Cheese shouted, patting his pizza dough hard and making even more flour fly up in the air. 'Look, I've made a face!' He held up his uncooked pizza. He had poked two eye holes and a big mouth hole in it.

'Jumping jellyfish, it looks just like Mr Tugg,' said Dad. And it did too.

Between us we managed to make THIRTY mini pizzas. Dad and I made most of them so they had decent toppings like ham and pineapple or red pepper, bacon and mozzarella. However, there were quite a few strange ones from the twins, like salami and chocolate, salami and crisps and salami and peanut butter. They seemed to like salami. I think it was because the word sounded funny.

After that the twins made gingerbread biscuits. Dad got out the pastry cutters and Tomato loved those, but Cheese wanted to make his own shapes. They turned out rather strange, but Cheese knew what they were if you asked.

'That's a shark and that one's a tree and there's a man with a gun hiding in it, and that one is a car crashing into another car and that one's a toilet.'

'Do you think people will want to eat a gingerbread toilet?' I asked him.

'No! It's a funny shape for laughing. Not to eat!' He obviously thought I was bonkers to even *think* anyone would want to *eat* it.

So we got all the pizzas and the gingerbread shapes made and they smelled lovely. The only

problem was that the kitchen now looked as if
a large troop of chimpanzees had come in and
gone bananas all over it, and I suppose that
wasn't that far from the truth.

By this time, Mum had finished sewing the
cloaks and she asked me if I'd like to go with her
to Mr and Mrs Wibbly's house to see if they liked
them and to make sure they fitted.

I had seen the Wibblys before but I had never
paid them any attention. I just thought they were
ever so old. Now I knew a bit more about them,
thanks to Granny, so I looked at them quite
carefully.

Mrs Wibbly was hardly any taller than me. She
was quite frail too. It was hard to imagine her
winning a gold medal. I told her what Granny
had said about the medal and Mrs Wibbly gave
me a lovely smile.

'It was a long time ago, dear,' she said. 'But it
did happen, and there's the medal. Up on that
wall there, see?'

'That's amazing,' I said, looking at the glittering medal and the photograph next to it. They were framed and behind glass. 'You were a champion!'

'She's still a champion,' said Mr Wibbly, putting an arm round his wife's shoulders.

Mum held up the two capes. 'Would you like to try them?'

'You sit down while we do this,' suggested Mrs Wibbly to me so I went and sat in one of the armchairs.

At least I *tried* to sit in an armchair, which had a big cushion plumped up on it, but as soon as I leaned back the cushion gave a surprised howl and leaped up. It was a cat! A big HUGELY fluffy grey cat.

'Don't mind Hartlepool,' said Mr Wibbly. 'He's always getting in the way.'

'That's an odd name for a cat,' said Mum as she put Mrs Wibbly's cape round the old lady's shoulders.

'It's the name of the town where I was born,' said Mr Wibbly. 'It always seemed a rather grey place to me as a child – the sea there was the same colour as Hartlepool's fur. He's very friendly.'

Hartlepool had recovered from the shock of me trying sit on him. We had a good cuddle and the cat lay across my lap purring like a helicopter while Mum made a few adjustments to the capes to get the length right.

'Are you looking forward to tomorrow?' I asked.

'To tell you the truth, Nicholas, I feel a bit embarrassed,' Mr Wibbly confessed.

'Why?'

'You see, my wife here has something special

she's done. She's an Olympic champion, but I've never done anything. I've worked most of my life, of course, but I've never done anything special. I feel as if I shouldn't really be there.'

'Listen to him talking nonsense!' cried Mrs Wibbly. 'He used to be a teacher!'

'But teaching is hugely important,' Mum declared. 'If there weren't any teachers the rest of us would be ignorant savages, wouldn't we, Nicholas?'

I just nodded, because what I was thinking was that if there weren't any teachers there'd be no school. And if there was no school I could play all the time and that would be – BRILLIANT! But I knew Mum was right. If I hadn't been taught I wouldn't be able to read or write or do maths or, well, ANYTHING! (Except possibly eat and breathe.)

'Being able to teach is a wonderful gift,' Mum said to Mr Wibbly.

'There,' Mrs Wibbly nodded. 'See? I've been

telling him that for years. My gold medal hasn't done anything useful, but you've given children the chance to make something of themselves. Now put that cape on and stop moaning!'

I liked Mr and Mrs Wibbly – and Hartlepool. We took the capes home so Mum could make the final alterations. That was when Mum discovered the kitchen.

Oh dear. She threw Dad out into the back garden and told him he was such a pig he should go and live with the other farm animals. She wouldn't let him back indoors until she'd finished cleaning, and I had to help.

'Look at this mess! I've never seen the like of it. And what's this meant to be?' Mum held up one of Cheese's gingerbread shapes.

'I think that one is meant to be a duck carrying a suitcase because it's going on holiday,' I explained, while Mum shook her head in disbelief.

'It's the last time I let any of you lot loose

in the kitchen to help with the cooking,' she growled.

But I knew it wouldn't be. I knew that, come the next day, Mum would be laughing about what had happened and it would all become a big joke. That's what our house is like, you see? A big joke. Well, most of the time, anyhow.

## 9. Bananas!

Today's the day! It's street-party day, and guess
what, we saw the news on TV this morning and
the Prince and Princess have had a baby. Well,
mostly it was the princess having the baby. I
think the prince just stood there and watched.
But guess what? There were TWO babies!
TWINS! Just like Cheese and Tomato. Now
everyone is waiting to hear what their names
will be.

'Silly sausage moo cow!' shouted Tomato.

'No,' I told her. 'The royal twins are not going
to be called silly sausage moo cow.'

Tomato sat back and blew a big raspberry at
me. Honestly, I don't know where she gets her
behaviour from. Oh, wait a minute, yes I do –
our dad! Sometimes *he's* just like a three-year-old!

Everyone is very excited, especially Mrs Quince-Porage. She's already standing out by her front gate, the one with the huge stone lions on either side – the lions that Dad always calls cowpats.

'They look ridiculous outside a house like that,' he said.

'I think you're jealous,' Mum chuckled. 'I bet you'd like a pair of lions by our front door.'

'Don't be ridiculous. Now, if you'd suggested a pair of lifesize hippos or a couple of gorillas that would be a different matter. They might frighten Mr Tugg away.'

Anyhow, Mrs Quince-Porage is out there because she's hoping to see Lady Gaga when she arrives. Ha ha! She's going to be in for a long wait!

We had a final rehearsal this morning and I reckon we sounded pretty good. My family is full of revelations – I love it! I wouldn't be the least bit startled if Granny turned out to be a pole-

vaulter like Mrs Wibbly. In fact, I hope I'm full of surprises when I grow up.

I still had a big worry on my mind, though. Charlie Smugg. What was he up to? Why did he have it in for the street party?

While The Bouncing Bandits were rehearsing there was a lot of activity on the road. Sergeant Smugg and his team had put yellow NO PARKING cones down both sides of the road, with the Sergeant measuring the space between each cone to make sure there was EXACTLY the same distance between each one. (Groan!)

The band had a short break so I took the twins out to watch the preparations. Several of our neighbours were putting up tables and setting out chairs. Others were covering tables with cloths. Mr Tugg marched up and down making sure everything was being done correctly. He stood on a chair and tested which way the wind was blowing, but I've no idea why.

Everyone was excited. They had all heard the

news. Royal twins! Everyone was wondering what they would be called.

'Cheese and Tomato!' said Cheese. He would, wouldn't he!

Mr Tugg began to turn red. 'You can't call a royal child Cheese or Tomato,' he said with undisguised disgust. 'Suppose the child becomes king one day? He'd be King Cheese. Ridiculous!'

He walked off in a huff, muttering to himself.

'King Cheese!' shouted Cheese, throwing out his arms as if he'd just come first in a race to be king. He turned to his sister. 'Queen Tomato!' They ran back indoors, giggling like crazy.

Indoors, The Bouncing Bandits were getting ready to have a final run-through and Dad was looking as if The End of The World was approaching fast.

'Mrs Quince-Porage is going to turn up soon, determined to sing,' he hissed. 'What are we going to do? We've got to stop her!'

Mum put down her drumsticks and folded her arms. 'You know, I thought it was odd that when Mrs Quince-Porage was here the other day she never asked us *why* Lady Gaga was at our house, and we never told her because it was just something Granny made up on the spot. Why don't we tell Mrs Quince-Porage that Lady Gaga was here to rehearse because she is going to sing at the party? Mrs Quince-Porage is hardly going to stop Lady Gaga from singing, is she?'

Dad grunted loudly. 'You're forgetting something, Brenda. We don't have Lady Gaga. That was Granny pretending to be her, and Granny will never be able to convince the whole street that she is Lady Gaga. Granny is a great double bass player, but she can't sing very well – can you, Gran?'

'No!' smiled Gran, and gave her double bass a big *TWANNGGGG!*

'I haven't finished what I was going to say,' said Mum when the others finally stopped muttering about Mrs Q-P and Granny. 'All we have to do is go on stage and let *you* sing, Ron. If Mrs Quince-Porage says anything we tell her that Lady Gaga had to pull out at the last minute because she got a nasty cold or something. By that time it will be too late for Mrs Quince-Porage to do anything.'

Dad threw down his guitar, leaped across the room and planted a big smacking kiss on Mum. 'You are a genius!' he cried. 'An absolute genius!

You have saved us from Mrs Quince-Porage.
Your name will go down in the history of this
street as a hero!'

'Don't be silly. We're not fighting a war,'
chuckled Mum.

'Oh yes we are!' chorused Dad, Granny and
Lancelot. 'WE have to stop that dreadful woman
singing, and you've done it. Three cheers for our
dazzling drummer!'

Mum seized her sticks and did a fanfare drum
roll to celebrate and we finished the rehearsal
feeling on top of the world.

Outside, everything was ready. The school had
allowed us to use its stage boxes and they had
been slotted together at the end of the street. The
Bouncing Bandits would be playing there and
two special chairs were also on it, decorated to
look like thrones. That was where Mr and Mrs
Wibbly would be crowned after they had passed
along the street with Sharon Blenkinsop, the
Crowning Maiden.

We raced through lunch because there was
still lots to do. Lancelot brought the cart round
for Rubbish the goat. He'd done it up really well,
so it only looked a little bit like a wheelbarrow.
The shafts, which he'd made from broomsticks,
fitted round the goat nicely, and Rubbish was
harnessed to the shafts with a few bits of soft
scarf. The barrow was decorated with shiny foil
and big cut-out flowers. There was just about
enough room for the twins and some of the hens.

I was worried about them jumping off and running away but Mum said that everyone in the street knew where they came from. 'If they find them they'll bring them back to us.'

Finally, Dad brought out the hat he'd made for Rubbish and put it carefully on her head. I don't think she was all that impressed. It was like a bonnet, but it had a large doll strapped to one side and an equally large cut-out of a baby stuck to the other.

'What on earth are those there for?' asked Mum.

'Those are the royal twins,' Dad told her. 'Don't you recognize them?'

'Idiot!' muttered Mum, but I could see she was laughing really.

That was about it. All we had to do now was get into our own costumes and we would be ready. We had been to visit a fancy-dress shop to help us out with some right royal clothes. Granny looked like a duchess, with a trailing floor-length

dress and loads of necklaces
and bracelets. She had a
little tiara on her head.

'Granny, you look great,'
I said. 'But how are you
going to play the double
bass?'

She gave me a mysterious
look. 'With my fingers of
course, like I always do.
All will be revealed, do not
worry, my little flower.'
She came towards me as
if she was going to kiss
me again, so I beat a
hasty retreat.

Mum was dressed as
the Queen of Hearts and
looked lovely. Lancelot
came as Sir
Lancelot, of course!

I was dressed as a jester, with a three-pronged hat and a bell on each prong. That just left Dad. He was gone a curiously long time. Maybe he was having trouble getting into his costume.

When he finally came downstairs we could see why. He could hardly move. That was because he was dressed as a giant banana.

Mum shrieked.
'Ron! You can't go
as a banana!'

'I can, and I shall,'
Dad said stiffly. 'Move
aside please so I can get
outside.' Dad stepped
out on to the street.
Behind him, we
followed, wondering
what on earth people
would think about
a giant banana
strolling down the
road.

'I wish I had your dad,' a voice said nearby. It
was Trevor, and he had Streaker with him. 'All
my dad does is play golf.' Trevor had come to
look after Rubbish for the parade. He helped pop
Cheese and Tomato on the cart and carry over a
couple of the hens.

'By the way, I've discovered what's up with Charlie,' Trevor said. 'Did you know he had a girlfriend?'

I shook my head.

'Sharon Blenkinsop. She dumped him a few days ago. Now she's going to do the crowning at your street party. Charlie is fuming at her. He's determined to get his revenge.'

'But what's he going to do?' I asked.

Trevor looked at me blankly and shook his head. 'Sorry. No idea at all. But you'd better watch out.'

## 10. Charlie Smugg Strikes!

The street was already filling with amazing costumes. There were kings and queens, and princes and princesses everywhere. I even saw Henry the Eighth on stilts. Some of the children were wearing really fancy stuff and looked incredibly smart. And then there were Cheese and Tomato, with tentacles, frills and goodness-knows-what down to their knees. Plus, the banana.

Mr Tugg, who was dressed as a royal servant, was outraged. 'It's an insult to the Queen!' he fumed, with steam starting to hiss from his ears. 'How dare you! In what way is a banana ANYTHING to do with the royal family?'

Dad coolly folded his arms. At least he tried to fold his arms but the banana costume made him too fat, so he pressed the tips of his fingers together instead and leaned forward a little. I think he was trying to look intelligent, but that's pretty difficult when you're dressed as a large banana.

'Mr Tugg, surely you know that bananas were first sold in this country in 1633, and they quickly became a favourite fruit of the royal family at the time. They were all the rage with Charles the First. I can assure you that bananas have been enjoyed by the royal family ever since. I am dressed like this as a tribute to the role of the banana in the royal family.'

With that, Dad turned away from Mr Tugg and marched off, immediately tripping over his own stalk and falling flat on his back. Mum snorted.

'I've seen people slip on a banana,' she said,
'but I've never seen a banana slip on itself. And
heaven knows how he's going to play his guitar.'

'He'll be fine,' Granny piped up. 'He's always
fine.'

At that moment a dazzling sight met our eyes.
It looked as if a gigantic meringue wearing an
outsize silver wig was floating towards us. It came
closer, and closer, and closer. It WAS a giant
meringue!

Well, maybe not quite. The meringue turned out to be Mrs Quince-Porage and she was wearing the most ginormously flouncy white dress and a ringletted silver wig was perched on top of her head, like one of those big round beehives, only made of hair. In fact, I half expected to see silver bees come zizzing out of it at any moment.

'DARLINGS!' she cried over the heads of the gathering crowd. 'I'M HERE! I'm here to sing!'

Mum instantly put on a dreadfully worried expression. Actually it was her I'm-so-sorry-to-tell-you-but-you're-not-wanted expression.

'What IS the matter?' dribbled Mrs Quince-Porage. 'Is something wrong?'

'Yes and no,' Mum began. 'You see, Lady Gaga has asked us if she can sing and, of course, we had to say "yes". I'm sure you understand. We could hardly turn down Lady Gaga.'

Mrs Quince-Porage shook her head and her wig wobbled alarmingly. 'Oh. OH! I was SO looking forward to singing, but of COURSE, you're right. Lady Gaga, HERE, in our little town, on OUR street! What an honour! Perhaps we could do a duet together!'

'Ah,' started Mum, and now she really did look worried. 'Maybe later on. Let's see how things go.'

'Oh GOODY!' beamed Mrs Quince-Porage.

'Until later then. In the meantime I must go and fetch the dessert I made for the street party. It's a chocolate mousse, darling. I ADORE chocolate mousse and this morning I made the biggest chocolate mousse ever. It should probably be in the *Guinness Book of Records*!'

'Splendid,' said Mum, nodding. 'Bye-bye.'

Off went Mrs Q-P. Mum turned to me and wiped her brow.

'Phew! Trust your father to disappear just when something awkward happens. How does he do that?'

'Practice,' said Granny. 'And he started young. I remember when he was three and he pulled a bowl of custard off the table and on to the floor. It was an accident, of course, but when I asked him if he'd done it he just stood there and pretended he was a tree.'

'A tree!' I was laughing already.

'Yes, Nicholas. A tree. He stood there with his arms up in the air and he looked straight at me and said 'I'm not Ronald. I'm a tree. It wasn't me, because I'm a tree.'

'Yes,' murmured Mum. 'And today he's a banana. Things don't change much, do they?'

We all burst into laughter then.

Lancelot was calling to us. 'Come on, hurry up, the parade has started. And, by the way, have you noticed all the press cameras? There's a film crew about somewhere too. We could end up on TV!'

We grabbed our instruments and launched into the first number, with Dad singing away at the front. He was quite possibly the first giant singing banana in history. We had a great view of everything, standing on the stage where the crowning was about to take place.

All the children came first, including Rubbish and the twin aliens, trailing tentacles in all directions. Streaker kept jumping up and trying to eat them – the tentacles that is, not the twins. Everyone was cheering and clapping. It was great. The committee sat at the side of the stage

and made notes about the children's costumes so that they could award prizes. Mr Tugg was there, of course, and the giant meringue and Sergeant Smugg too.

Last of all in the procession was a wonderful vintage car, polished until it sparkled like the crown jewels. It was an open-top car and sitting in the back were Mr and Mrs Wibbly on their way to be crowned. With them was Sharon

Blenkinsop, grinning madly at everyone and waving both her hands as if she was the star of the show, not Mr and Mrs Wibbly. Even so, the old couple didn't seem to mind. I guess they were just too nice to say anything.

The car stopped beside the stage. The driver got out and opened both the rear doors. Out came Mr and Mrs Wibbly wearing their glorious capes that my mum had made for them.

Then came Sharon, still waving at everyone
and curtseying and looking for cameras that
she could pose for. The Wibblys mounted the
stairs to the stage and sat on their thrones, with
Sharon between them, grinning like a toothpaste
advertisement.

Now that everyone was in place for the main
event The Bouncing Bandits stopped playing so
the next, most important part of the afternoon
could take place.

Everyone gathered at the foot of the stage:
all the children and their mums and dads and
grannies and grandads and aunts and uncles.
Everybody was there waiting for the crowning.

This was to be Sharon Blenkinsop's moment
of glory. She picked up the first crown, raised
it high into the air, and slowly brought it down
and placed in on King Wibbly the First's head. A
chorus of 'Hooray!' thundered into the sky and
there was lots of wild clapping. Sharon picked up
the second crown.

At that moment, I looked out over the cheering crowd and glimpsed something that froze my heart on the spot. Right at the back of everyone, keeping his spotty head down, was Charlie Smugg. In a flash I knew trouble was coming but I had no idea what or how. There was nothing I could do.

Charlie's head suddenly bobbed up again. His right arm went back, about to throw something, and then he flung it as hard and as far as he could, straight over the crowd and towards the stage. A tennis ball. And then another tennis ball, and another!

And behind the tennis balls came three leaping, snarling, snapping Alsatians! It was CHAOS!

Screams, shouts and yells split the air. The dogs came pounding through the crowd, scattering people in all directions. As some tried to run away they collided with others. People fell to the ground and then more people tripped over them. Soon the crowd became a heaving mass of bodies, and the dogs – the snarling, snapping Alsatians – were getting closer and closer. They

reached the cart. Rubbish was scared out of his wits and went crashing off, scattering more of the crowd. Cheese and Tomato hung on for dear life as they bounced about all over the place.

Charlie's dogs came bounding up the stage, still chasing the tennis balls. Over went King Wibbly as his chair tipped backwards. Sharon Blenkinsop was knocked completely off her feet and the crown she was holding went spinning up, up, up in the air.

I watched, mesmerized, as the crown somersaulted through the air, slowed, stopped and then began to spin back down to earth. At the same moment, Rubbish and the cart came careering past the stage. Cheese had been jiggled and juggled until he was upside down, but he was still clinging on, his little bottom sticking into the air. And then – *PLOP!* – down came the crown and landed – *PLUMMP!* – upon his bum! And stuck there!

Off went Rubbish, the cart, Tomato and Cheese, with Cheese's backside bouncing up and down and the crown stuck firmly upon it. All of a sudden my little brother was King Cheese-Bottom!

Meanwhile, the dogs were rooting all over the stage for the tennis balls. Granny had climbed up her double bass to get away from them. Mum was noisily beating her biggest drum to scare them away. Dad was hiding inside his banana costume. And then, who should come to our rescue? You will never guess.

Hartlepool. Yes, the Wibblys' cat! All of sudden this monster appeared. He was huge. He was scary. He was Hartlepool. All his great mass of fur was on end. He was hissing like a nest of snakes. The first Alsatian came too close and *ZZZSWICE*! In a lightning flash a single paw, complete with claw, shot out and got the dog on the nose.

*OWOWOWOWOWOW!* You've never heard
such an agonized yelp. The dog was off in a trice,
followed by the other two and behind them was
Hartlepool, chasing all three Alsatians down the
road until they disappeared.

People were slowly getting to their feet. I
noticed Charlie sneaking round the edge of the
crowd to get to his dogs. I saw Sharon Blenkinsop
stagger to her feet and see him. She looked at

him. He looked at her. Sharon's arm shot out, pointing an accusing finger at him.

'Charlie Smugg!' she screeched. 'I know it was you what did this! I'll get you, Charlie! Just you wait and see!'

She leaped from the stage into the crowd and began charging towards him. Charlie was off in a flash. The crowd started to laugh. Charlie the bully boy was fleeing for his life – from a girl! He was as much a coward as his Alsatians.

Dad was laughing his head off. 'Brilliant!' he yelled. 'The best street party I've ever been to. Come on, let's play!'

So we set to with a rousing dance number and soon the party was in full flow again. Trevor managed to catch up with Rubbish and bring back the goat. We retrieved the crown from Cheese's bottom and placed it solemnly on Queen Wibbly's head.

Everything was fine and dandy once more.

And that was when Mrs Quince-Porage

appeared, carrying an enormous chocolate mousse.

'But WHERE is Lady Gaga?' she cried. 'Has she not turned up? You have no singer. I MUST come to your rescue. Oh, I must, MUST SING!'

And she made her way up the steps towards us.

## 11. Chapter the Last

Mrs Quince-Porage came hurrying up the steps to the stage, bearing her enormous chocolate mousse in front of her. She reached the top step and, just at that moment, a happy, yappy, over-excited and HUNGRY black dog came hurtling out of the crowd and up the steps behind her. Suddenly, Mrs Q-P and her mousse were flying forward. Down they both went, with Streaker riding Mrs Q-P's back and then they hit the stage:

BANNGGGG!!

SPERR – LAPPPPPPP!!!

Yes, Mrs Quince-Porage fell face first into her own mousse! The band stopped. The crowd went silent. Everyone peered forward.

Mrs Q-P lay stretched out and still. Seconds

passed. Then she began to shake her
head. Streaker started licking chocolate
out of her wig. She struggled to her
knees. Chocolate dripped from her nose,
her ears, her chin, her whole upper body
really. She had become a chocolate giant,

or maybe a giant chocolate, or even both.

'My mousse!' wailed Mrs Quince-Porage.

'Quick!' cried Dad. 'One, two, three –' And
The Bouncing Bandits launched into 'Food,
Glorious Food.'

And that was it really. The street party settled down to eating and feasting and dancing and it all went on until almost midnight. It was brilliant. Everyone enjoyed themselves so much that a few began using Sergeant Smugg's NO PARKING cones as hats. I don't think the sergeant was very pleased, but he kept his handcuffs to himself and just scowled.

The next day there were some great photos in the newspapers and we were even on television. The TV crew had filmed all the chaos too and that really made the news, especially the bit where Cheese's bottom got crowned! That came out really well on TV.

But you'll never guess in a million years what happened after that, so I will tell you. About four days after the street party there was a knock at the door and who was there – Mr Tugg. He didn't look all that happy either.

'I received a letter today from the palace,' said Mr Tugg, waving a big white envelope.

'Goodness,' said Dad. 'Are you going to knighted, Mr Tugg?'

'Of course not, don't be ridiculous.'

'Well, are you going to be executed then?'

Mr Tugg drew himself up to his full height, which wasn't a lot. 'I know you think you're funny, but you're not,' he told Dad bluntly. 'I have a letter from the Queen's secretary thanking the committee, of which I am –'

'Deputy chairman,' Dad said, sighing.

'Exactly. Deputy chairman. Thanking the committee for providing wonderful entertainment, not just for the street, but for the whole country.'

'Really?'

'Yes. Along with that letter came this envelope which is addressed to "*The family with the royal bottom*". I believe they must be referring to you and your small son. There!'

Mr Tugg handed the envelope to Dad. He was obviously seething with annoyance that we should get a royal letter as well as the committee.

Dad took the envelope and studied it. On the back was a big red seal carrying the imprint of the royal arms.

'What does it say, Dad? Open it!' I was *so* excited!

Dad ripped it open with one finger. He pulled out a piece of folded paper, opened it up and read it.

> *Dear family,*
>
> *The Prince and Princess would like to thank you for the wonderful entertainment you provided on the television news. We were fascinated to learn that you have twins called Cheese and Tomato. As you know, the Princess has recently given birth to twins herself. They will be called Rupert and Alexandra. However, in honour of Cheese's royal bottom we have decided that our twins will unofficially be known to us as Ham and Pineapple.*
>
> *Yours royally,*
>
> *The Prince and Princess*

Mr Tugg staggered back as Dad read out the letter.

'Ham and Pineapple!' he stuttered. 'Prince

Ham and Princess Pineapple! You can't call royal babies Ham and Pineapple. The world's gone mad. I think I'm going to explode! I am going to explode. Yes, I can feel it. Here it comes. AAAAAAARGHH! RAAARRRRRRFGGH!!'

Off he went, spinning down the road with steam coming out of his ears, his nose and more than likely his bottom as well.

That's Mr Tugg for you. I told you he's like a volcano. Byeeeee!

## Ask Jeremy

## Of all the books you have written, which one is your favourite?

I loved writing both **KRAZY KOW SAVES THE WORLD – WELL, ALMOST** and **STUFF**, my first book for teenagers. Both these made me laugh out loud while I was writing and I was pleased with the overall result in each case. I also love writing the stories about Nicholas and his daft family – **MY DAD**, **MY MUM**, **MY BROTHER** and so on.

## If you couldn't be a writer what would you be?

Well, I'd be pretty fed up for a start, because writing was the one thing I knew I wanted to do from the age of nine onward. But if I DID have to do something else, I would love to be either an accomplished pianist or an artist of some sort. Music and art have played a big part in my whole life and I would love to be involved in them in some way.

## What's the best thing about writing stories?

Oh dear – so many things to say here! Getting paid for making things up is pretty high on the list! It's also something you do on your own, inside your own head – nobody can interfere with that. The only boss you have is yourself. And you are creating something that nobody else has made before you. I also love making my readers laugh and want to read more and more.

## Did you ever have a nightmare teacher?
## (And who was your best ever?)

My nightmare at primary school was Mrs Chappell, long since dead. I knew her secret – she was not actually human. She was a Tyrannosaurus rex in disguise. She taught me for two years when I was in Y5 and Y6, and we didn't like each other at all. My best ever was when I was in Y3 and Y4. Her name was Miss Cox, and she was the one who first encouraged me to write stories. She was brilliant. Sadly, she is long dead too.

## When you were a kid you used to play kiss-chase. Did you always do the chasing or did anyone ever chase you?!

I usually did the chasing, but when I got chased, I didn't bother to run very fast! Maybe I shouldn't admit to that! We didn't play kiss-chase at school – it was usually played during holidays. If we had tried playing it at school we would have been in serious trouble. Mind you, I seemed to spend most of my time in trouble of one sort or another, so maybe it wouldn't have mattered that much.

# LAUGH YOUR SOCKS OFF WITH Jeremy STRONG

Jeremy Strong has written SO many books to make you laugh your socks right off. There are the Streaker books and the Famous Bottom books and the Pyjamas books and . . . PHEW!

Welcome to the JEREMY STRONG FAMILY TREE, which shows you all of Jeremy's brilliant books in one easy-to-follow-while-laughing-your-socks-off way!

## MY BROTHER'S FAMOUS BOTTOM

Nicholas's baby brother, Cheese, is famous. Well, his bottom is, because he advertises Dumper disposable nappies . . .

## THE HUNDRED-MILE-AN-HOUR DOG

Streaker is no ordinary dog; she's a rocket on four legs with a woof attached . . .

## COSMIC PYJAMAS

Pyjamas are just pyjamas, right? Not when they're COSMIC PYJAMAS, swooooosh! . . .

# 14½ Things You Didn't Know About

# Jeremy Strong

★ ★ ★ ★ ★ ★ ★ ★ ★ ★ ★ ★ ★ ★ ★ ★ ★ ★ ★ ★ ★

1. He loves eating liquorice.

2. He used to like diving. He once dived from the high board and his trunks came off!

3. He used to play electric violin in a rock band called **THE INEDIBLE CHEESE SANDWICH**.

4. He got a 100-metre swimming certificate when he couldn't even swim.

5. When he was five, he sat on a heater and burnt his bottom.

6. Jeremy used to look after a dog that kept eating his underpants. (No – **NOT** while he was wearing them!)

7. When he was five, he left a basin tap running with the plug in and flooded the bathroom.

8. He can make his ears waggle.

9. He has visited over a thousand schools.

10. He once scored minus ten in an exam! That's ten less than nothing!

11. His hair has gone grey, but his mind hasn't.

12. He'd like to have a pet tiger.

13. He'd like to learn the piano.

14. He has dreadful handwriting.

**And a half . . .** His favourite hobby is sleeping. He's very good at it.

# Bright and shiny and sizzling with fun stuff . . .

# puffin.co.uk

## WEB FUN

**UNIQUE and exclusive digital content!**
Podcasts, photos, Q&A, Day in the Life of, interviews
and much more, from Eoin Colfer, Cathy Cassidy,
Allan Ahlberg and Meg Rosoff to Lynley Dodd!

## WEB NEWS

The **Puffin Blog** is packed with posts and photos from
Puffin HQ and special guest bloggers. You can also sign up
to our monthly newsletter **Puffin Beak Speak**

## WEB CHAT

**Discover something new** EVERY month –
books, competitions and treats galore

## WEBBED FEET

(Puffins have funny little feet and
brightly coloured beaks)

# Point your mouse our way today!

# It all started with a Scarecrow.

### Puffin is seventy years old.
Sounds ancient, doesn't it? But Puffin has never been
so lively. We're always on the lookout for the next big
idea, which is how it began all those years ago.

Penguin Books was a big idea from the mind of
a man called Allen Lane, who in 1935 invented
the quality paperback and changed the world.
**And from great Penguins, great Puffins grew,
changing the face of children's books forever.**

The first four Puffin Picture Books were hatched in 1940 and the
first Puffin story book featured a man with broomstick arms called
Worzel Gummidge. In 1967 Kaye Webb, Puffin Editor, started the
Puffin Club, promising to **'make children into readers'**.
She kept that promise and over 200,000 children became
devoted Puffineers through their quarterly instalments of
*Puffin Post*, which is now back for a new generation.

Many years from now, we hope you'll look back and
remember Puffin with a smile. **No matter what your age
or what you're into, there's a Puffin for everyone.**
The possibilities are endless, but one thing is for sure:
whether it's a picture book or a paperback, a sticker book
or a hardback, **if it's got that little Puffin
on it – it's bound to be good.**